For Olivia
—Aldous Huxley, 1944

For my father,
Simon Blackall, with love
— Sophie Blackall, 2011

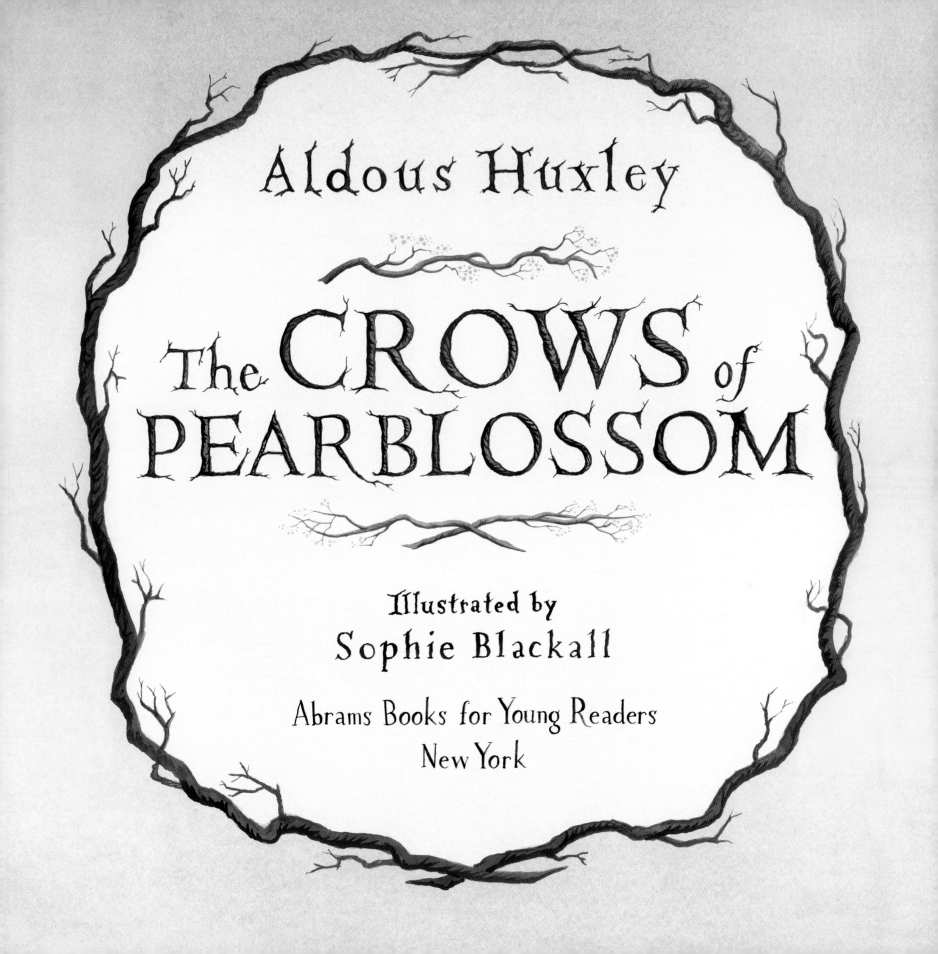

Aldous Huxley

The CROWS of PEARBLOSSOM

Illustrated by
Sophie Blackall

Abrams Books for Young Readers
New York

Once upon a time there were two crows who had a nest in a cottonwood tree at Pearblossom.

In a hole at the bottom of the tree lived a Rattlesnake. He was very old and very big and when he shook his rattles the noise was so loud that it could be heard by the children at school in Littlerock.

Most of the time he slept but every afternoon punctually at half past three, he used to crawl out of his hole, climb the tree and look into the crow's nest.

If there was an egg in the nest—which there generally was—he would swallow it in one mouthful, shell and all. Then he crawled back into his hole and went to sleep again.

When Mrs. Crow came back from the store where she went every afternoon to buy her groceries, she would find the nest empty. "What can have happened to my darling little egg?" she would say as she hunted high and low. But she never found it; so after tea she laid another one.

This had gone on for a long time when, one day, Mrs. Crow came home earlier than usual and caught Mr. Snake in the act of swallowing her latest egg.

"Monster!" she cried. "What are you doing?"

Speaking with his mouth full, the snake answered: "I'm having breakfast." And he glided down the tree and into his hole.

When Mr. Crow came home that evening from Palmdale, where he worked as Assistant Manager in the drugstore, he found his wife looking very pale and haggard, pacing up and down the branch outside their nest.

"What's the matter, Amelia?" he said. "You look quite ill. You haven't been overeating again, have you?"

"How can you be so coarse and unfeeling?" Mrs. Crow burst out. "Here am I, working myself to the bone for you; when I'm not working, laying a fresh egg every single day—except Sundays, of course, and public holidays—two hundred and ninety-seven eggs a year, and not a single chick hatched out. And all you can do is ask if I've been overeating. And when I think of that dreadful snake, I go all of a tremble."

"Snake?" said Mr. Crow. "What snake?"

"The one that ate all my darling little eggs," said Mrs. Crow, and once again burst into tears.

When at last she was able to explain what had happened, Mr. Crow shook his head. "This is serious," he said. "This is the sort of thing that somebody will have to do something about."

"Why don't you go down into the snake's hole and kill him?" asked Mrs. Crow.

"Somehow, I don't feel that that's a very good idea," Mr. Crow answered.

"Abraham, you're scared!" said Mrs. Crow.

"Scared?" repeated Mr. Crow. "I never said I was scared. All I said was that I didn't think your idea was a very good one. Your ideas are seldom good, I may add. That's why I shall go and talk to my friend Owl. Owl's a thinker. His ideas are always good."

So he flew off to the tall poplar in Mr. Yost's garden, where Old Man Owl had his home. Old Man Owl, who worked on a night shift and slept all day, was just getting up when Mr. Crow knocked at his door.

"Come in, Abraham," he said. "Excuse my being in bedroom slippers."

Mr. Crow took a seat, and while Old Man Owl shaved and combed his feathers, he told him the whole story.

"Well," said Old Man Owl, when he had finished, "there's obviously only one thing to be done."

"What's that?"

"Wait and see."

And with that, Old Man Owl opened the door and flew down into the middle of Mr. Yost's alfalfa patch, which had been irrigated that day and was still quite wet.

"Oh, it's all muddy," said Mr. Crow as he landed beside his friend.

"Abraham, you talk too much," said Old Man Owl. "Keep your beak shut and do exactly what I do."

So saying, he took a big handful of mud and began to shape it into the form of an egg. Mr. Crow did the same, and when they had finished, Old Man Owl flew up to the roof of Olivia's house, just where the chimney came up from the living room. The stove was burning and the chimney was very hot. Old Man Owl dropped the two eggs into an old tin can and placed the can on the top of the chimney.

Then the two friends flew back to Owl's house and had supper. By the time they had finished washing up and listened to the evening concert on the radio, it was ten o'clock and the moon was shining brightly over the mountains.

"I guess those eggs will be cooked by now," said Old Man Owl.

So they flew back again to the chimney, and sure enough, the clay eggs had baked through and through and were as hard as stone.

"What color are your wife's eggs?" asked Old Man Owl.

"Pale green," said Mr. Crow, "with small black spots."

"Well, it's lucky that Siggy has been doing some painting around the place," said Old Man Owl.

And, taking the can with the eggs, he flew down to the table outside the kitchen door where there were several pots of paints and some brushes. When the eggs had been painted so as to look exactly like real eggs, Old Man Owl and Mr. Crow dried them over the chimney, and then, about midnight, when the paint was quite hard, they flew back to the old cottonwood tree, where Mrs. Crow was impatiently waiting for them.

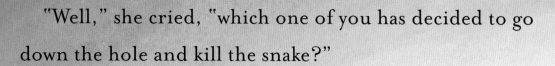

"Well," she cried, "which one of you has decided to go down the hole and kill the snake?"

"Neither of us," said Mr. Crow.

"Neither of you?" screamed Mrs. Crow. "Then must two hundred and ninety-seven of my darling eggs disappear down that vile serpent's throat? Must my heart go on being broken, day after day, forever?"

"Amelia," said Mr. Crow, "you talk too much. Keep your
beak shut and get out of your nest."

Mrs. Crow did as she was told and Old Man Owl took the
eggs out of the can and placed them in the nest.

"What are those for?" asked Mrs. Crow.

"Wait and see," said Old Man Owl; and with that he flew
off toward Llano, where he had an appointment with a
friend to go gopher hunting.

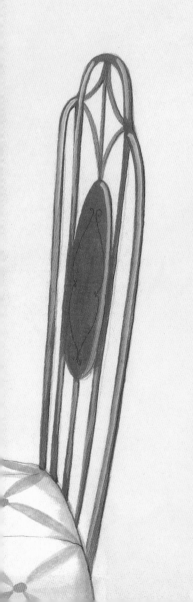

Next Afternoon

Mrs. Crow went down to the store as usual to do her shopping. While she was gone, Mr. Snake woke up and, feeling hungry, came gliding out of his hole, up the tree, and along the branch to Mr. and Mrs. Crow's nest.

"Two eggs today!" he said; "nyum—nyum." And he smacked his lips, for his mother neglected his education and he had very bad manners. Then he stuck out his neck and swallowed the two eggs whole, first one and then the other.

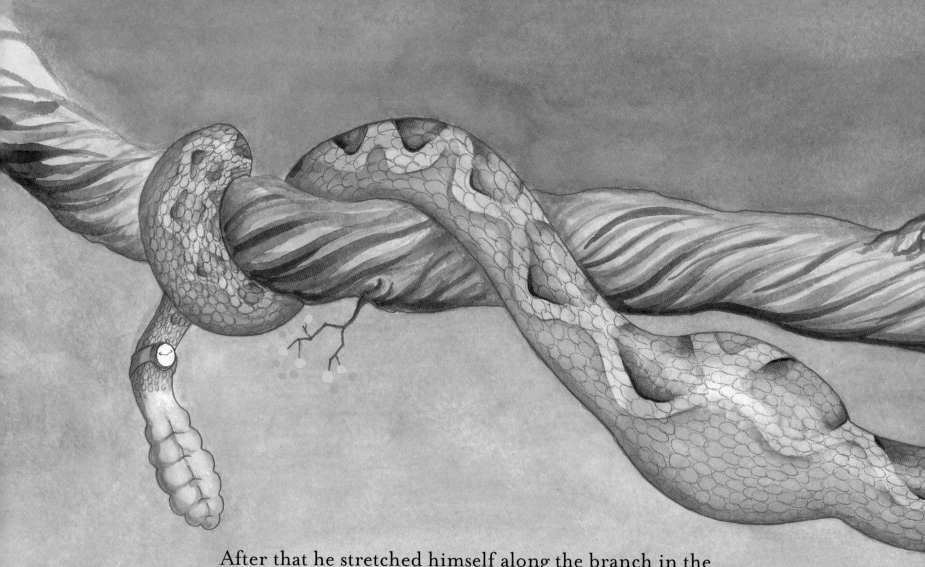

After that he stretched himself along the branch in the
sunshine and began to sing a little song.

I cannot fly—I have no wings;

I cannot run—I have no legs;

But I can creep where the blackbird sings

And eat her speckled eggs, ha, ha,

And eat her speckled eggs.

Suddenly he broke off. "Those eggs must have had very
thick shells," he said to himself.

"Generally they break before they even get to my stomach.
But this time it seems to be different." All at once he began
to have the most frightful stomachache. "Ow," he said.
"Ooh, aie, eeh." But the stomachache only got worse and
worse. "Ow, ooh, aie." Mr. Snake began to writhe and
wriggle and twist and turn.

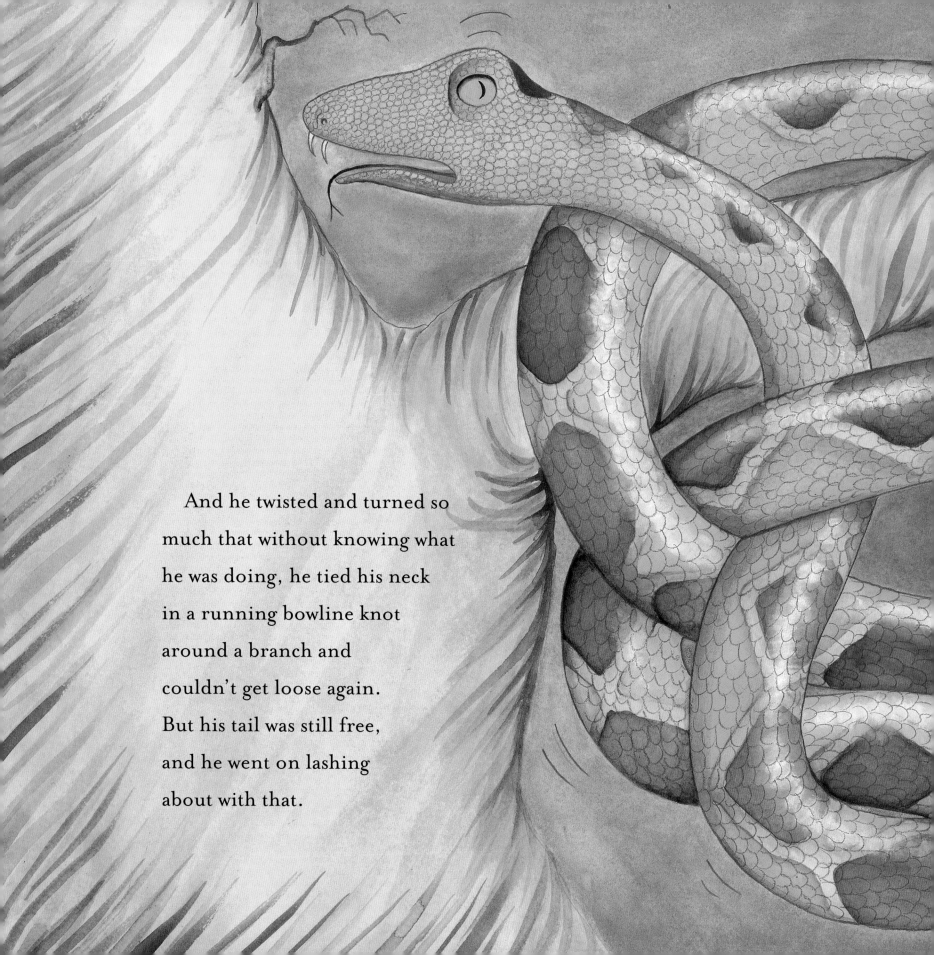

And he twisted and turned so
much that without knowing what
he was doing, he tied his neck
in a running bowline knot
around a branch and
couldn't get loose again.
But his tail was still free,
and he went on lashing
about with that.

And he lashed so furiously, he coiled and corkscrewed into such complicated convulsions that at last he got his tail tied up in a clove hitch around another branch of the tree. So there he was and the harder he tried to get loose, the tighter the knot became. And all the time the clay eggs in his insides were giving him the most excruciating stomachache.

By and by Mrs. Crow came back from the store, and at first, when she saw the snake, she was frightened. But as soon as she noticed how tightly he had tied himself up she felt very brave and proceeded to give the snake a very long lecture on the wickedness of eating other people's eggs.

Since that time Mrs. Crow has

successfully hatched out four families of seventeen

children each. And she uses the snake as a clothesline

on which to hang the little crows' diapers.

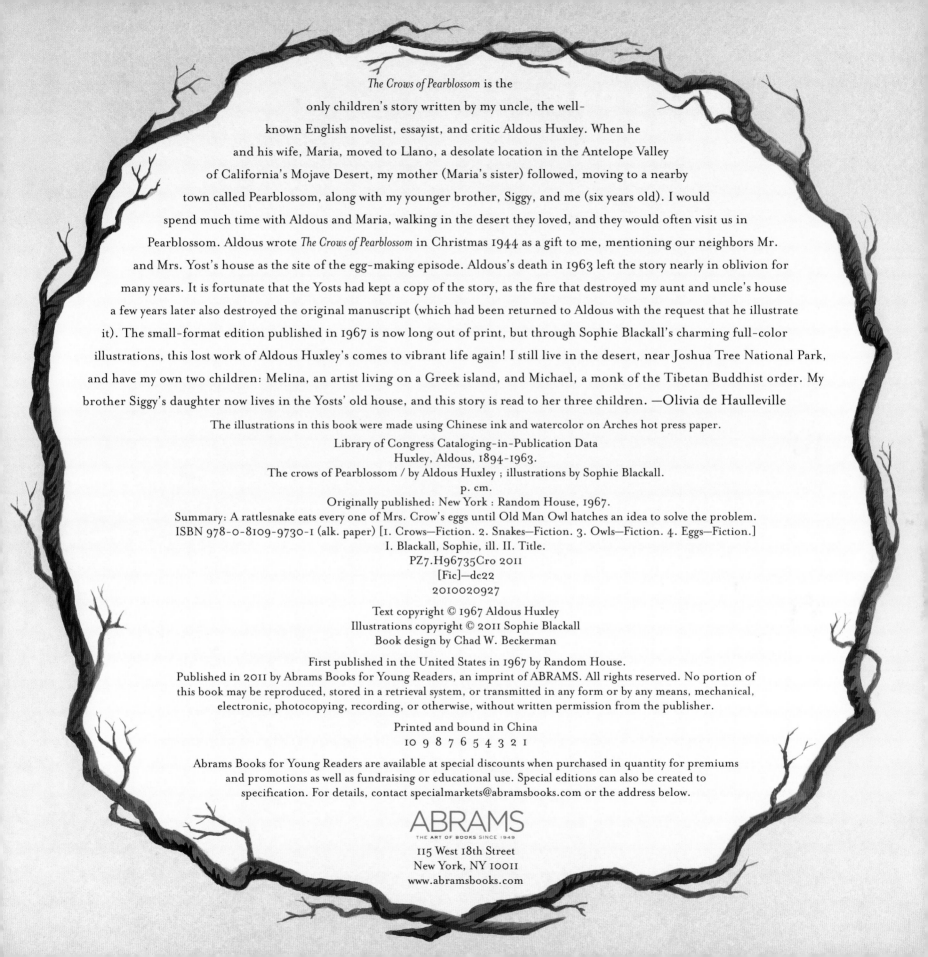

The Crows of Pearblossom is the only children's story written by my uncle, the well-known English novelist, essayist, and critic Aldous Huxley. When he and his wife, Maria, moved to Llano, a desolate location in the Antelope Valley of California's Mojave Desert, my mother (Maria's sister) followed, moving to a nearby town called Pearblossom, along with my younger brother, Siggy, and me (six years old). I would spend much time with Aldous and Maria, walking in the desert they loved, and they would often visit us in Pearblossom. Aldous wrote *The Crows of Pearblossom* in Christmas 1944 as a gift to me, mentioning our neighbors Mr. and Mrs. Yost's house as the site of the egg-making episode. Aldous's death in 1963 left the story nearly in oblivion for many years. It is fortunate that the Yosts had kept a copy of the story, as the fire that destroyed my aunt and uncle's house a few years later also destroyed the original manuscript (which had been returned to Aldous with the request that he illustrate it). The small-format edition published in 1967 is now long out of print, but through Sophie Blackall's charming full-color illustrations, this lost work of Aldous Huxley's comes to vibrant life again! I still live in the desert, near Joshua Tree National Park, and have my own two children: Melina, an artist living on a Greek island, and Michael, a monk of the Tibetan Buddhist order. My brother Siggy's daughter now lives in the Yosts' old house, and this story is read to her three children. —Olivia de Haulleville

The illustrations in this book were made using Chinese ink and watercolor on Arches hot press paper.

Library of Congress Cataloging-in-Publication Data
Huxley, Aldous, 1894–1963.
The crows of Pearblossom / by Aldous Huxley ; illustrations by Sophie Blackall.
p. cm.
Originally published: New York : Random House, 1967.
Summary: A rattlesnake eats every one of Mrs. Crow's eggs until Old Man Owl hatches an idea to solve the problem.
ISBN 978-0-8109-9730-1 (alk. paper) [1. Crows—Fiction. 2. Snakes—Fiction. 3. Owls—Fiction. 4. Eggs—Fiction.]
I. Blackall, Sophie, ill. II. Title.
PZ7.H96735Cro 2011
[Fic]—dc22
2010020927

Text copyright © 1967 Aldous Huxley
Illustrations copyright © 2011 Sophie Blackall
Book design by Chad W. Beckerman

First published in the United States in 1967 by Random House.

Printed and bound in China
10 9 8 7 6 5 4 3 2 1

ABRAMS
THE ART OF BOOKS SINCE 1949
115 West 18th Street
New York, NY 10011
www.abramsbooks.com

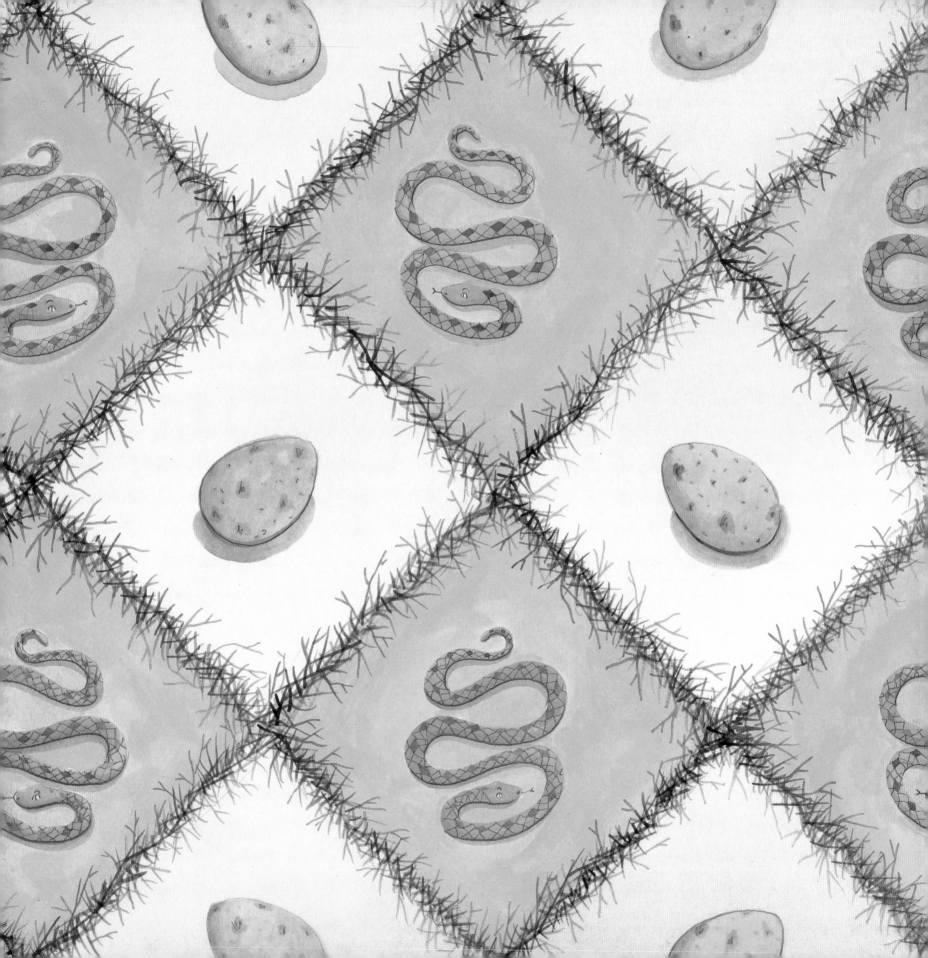